Gifts to the Gods of the floor

Shelley Eastwick

Mims and the Moon

www.mimsandthemoon.com

"There was a star riding through clouds one night, and I said to the star, 'Consume me'.

Virginia Woolf, The Waves

"I thrive best hermit style, with a beard and a pipe."

Bjork, Unison

"Fucking Ada!"

My Mum, several times a day

Contents:

<u>Poems from the Midnight Oil series</u>

Heirloom:

I wake up

never realising that the 22s I chase

are attached to the tail of my very own traveller's coat.

And then I suddenly stop

or fall

or perhaps I push myself.

Either way, I always land like a gift to the Gods of the floor

and with my same old thud realise that

I am tangled up in lore.

Floating towards a dark spot on the sun,

the pupiled centre of my own pain

blinks back at me

and I am forced to watch the

crumbling

of my self-fulfilling fantasy.

You see, I have grasped a handful of nettles fully drenched in

midnight oil

and I have sung silver songs so sticky green icky

that it makes my wandering mind recoil.

But trying to slow my descent

is like trying to catch a shooting star,

for I always know that I am meant to seek

the depths that they warn are too far.

I need you to know that I am never wishing for death.

It's sadder.

It's oh so much harder to achieve.

I yearn so desperately for more life -

dancing in the salt mist of the sea.

You see, I think I am a vast desert

but the grains of sand I pad along

are actually part of an hourglass

I hold in the palm of my hand.

Always sipping my Jesus juice

and never stopping to understand.

This is my pattern.

This is my patchwork quilted heirloom

I pass onto myself every time there is a circus sky,

celebrating the circles of my mind

whilst four and twenty of my dreams are

baked in a pie.

And then so slowly

and perhaps almost religiously,

I move my hand towards the deviating rainbow beam I tiptoe along

– a beam I repeatedly sketch with my own pencil,

and I whisk away all it has to offer.

I become like quicksand and

sink

so deeply into myself

that I can feel my very existence fragmenting.

I am breaking away.

Fragments of myself fall from me

as quickly

and as easily

as the dresses of a whore

and I finally come to realise that

I can trust myself no more.

Then, just as rapidly as the holes within me appear

I fill them with pistachio-shaded oil

so sweet

a sticky tapestry stitching over the fears.

Constantly folding back into myself

I collage

cut and paste, artificially recreate

until it is like revisiting the scene of a crime

that never took place.

Fingernails:

Under her fingernails, like sand.
She digs deep and watches the grains separate and fuse,
her fingertips raining gold.
A cascade of dreams fountain from her palms
he is under her fingernails, like sand.

Penetrating her each and every pore
he spins a thirsty con.
Lapping the air desperately as he exhales
she drinks the dew that ripples from his breath.
He moves within her
she absorbs.
In her blood, like heroin.

Beneath her skin he meanders
scouting for places to keep.
Enveloping every fibre of her being in a soporific haze
he creeps to her like sleep.
In her blood, like an antidote.

Wrapped around her, like a garment
his silk mummifies her senses.
Gliding into every crevasse of her landscape
he dresses her in webs of reassurance.
Wrapped around her body, like a deviant cocoon.

Under her fingernails, like sand.

Like dust lifted by a gentle breeze

he settles over her -

a blanket of illusions wishing away the strains of time.

She digs deep and watches the grains.

He is under her fingernails, like sand.

☾

The Grassy Meadow:

She is only an acid teardrop away from their heaven

and a rose-tinted one away from hers.

Here she sits

at her window to the world

only ever looking upwards.

She does not see the ageing lady

stereotypically twitching her curtains across the way

and she ignores the stonewash jeans

hanging

out of the window opposite.

She instead looks upwards.

Her eyes burning into the only jigsaw piece of sky visible

through the landscape of brickwork,

until she can see right through it and beyond.

When beyond;

when she has finally managed to claw her way through

the big smoke screen

whose hand covers her mouth,

she can see rainbow spangled ribbons of light

emanating from Mary Jane's smile

to ease the rest of the way.

This is a sideward glance

at the carefully hidden burdens

and achingly parched mind

of Miss Alice B. Toke -

one of those complex slim blue types

we read about each time the moon sighs

and who we feel compelled to use spears of

pity, waste and expectation

in reference to thereafter.

She is the type of girl that often screams so silently

that only the unborn can hear her,

which explains why they scream, plead

in protest

when forced to arrive.

When Miss Toke opens her mouth

an unintelligible mesh of global disease

and shattered astral insights

spill over

from the confused wash of her brain;

society's venom stinging her eyes

in gleeful hope

that the final drop will make her

fall

to their ground.

It is always at this point,

when her breath turns into life defining chinese whispers,

that Miss Toke manically searches for a needle

of space outside of the haystack

she is tangled up in.

Thrashing forcefully through the final web

of misleading thorns

with her bruised abused misused body,

Alice enters Mary's wonderland.

Mary's extended gloved hand,

like a gift-wrapped antidote,

leads Miss Toke through the grassy meadow:

Where the trees sigh for her every time

she flows past them

on a different stream of time;

the scorched earth accepts her grief

and the whistling wisdom of the wind

lullabies all of her dangling threads

into a soporific permanence of sleep.

Laying down

Miss Toke lets the arms of the meadow support her.

Blades of grass jig and jive around her face

and her thoughts become like a parade of butterflies:

fluttering in quick succession

from one desolation row

of the labyrinth

to another.

Spiralling her towards finally, fully

understanding herself

her surroundings and beyond.

Kneeling beside her

Mary Jane pours warm oil

drained from the wisest parts of the cosmos

in to Alice's once disillusioned ear.

A golden green and brown cocktail.

An escape route

blended from sacred ingredients

and passed through the hands of four generations of

females with wishing-stars for eyes.

Watching Miss Toke sip from Mary's majestically brimming flute,

you might – just for a moment,

think she was instead dancing barefoot in a city fountain

with her head thrown back

in fits of reefergiggles.

The rats break from the race long enough to

stare

tut

judge

and disapprove,

yet the very core of them yearns

for her ability to splash and smile so flirtatiously

at the subliminal strangers

and dangers of the unknown.

Her freedom-giggle bubbles through the air

lightly brushing each and every cheek of the crowd

with sad realisations

and breath-gulping truth;

making them feel – just for a moment –

like they've been kissed by an angel with broken wings.

But you would be mistaken:

for Miss Toke is not dancing in one of the squares of the grid,

but on that line that separates them.

Trapeze walking along the border

that differentiates one grid square

from the other -

moon walking in that space that exists in between words.

To the eyes around her it appears that the pipe she smokes

is packed with her dreams;

with every breath one is lost,

burnt out,

goes up in smoke.

But come closer.

Focus on her until the hidden picture jumps out,

magic eye trickery

waiting to be visually deciphered.

Notice how the heated earth scalding her fingertips

sadistically reassures her

that she's not completely numb.

She still manages to pick the pocket of the timekeeper

and steal moments drenched in honey

amid the social lockdown.

Crumbling the squidgy black parts of her memory

into golden dust,

the pipe she smokes is instead made of her past -

each cherry spark the last glow

of the parts of her that hurt,

igniting her future as they fall to the ground.

Untouched, untainted, unjudged and understood

when Mary blows smoke-rings

of sacred clarity her way.

Using mirrors and cats and broomsticks and bees

she dismantles

the buds of knowledge:

scattering them around her like party confetti

and then collaging the torn pieces

into a more digestible form.

Rearranging the faces and places and numbers and letters

until the world becomes a turquoise pill

that she can swallow with ease.

Enabling her to cradle – just for a moment –

the control, creativity and completion

she weeps for at her window stained with tears.

Miss Toke is so high that she can hear heaven.

☾

Goldfish:

Drifting towards the edge of the murky canvass
that they need,
her flame-tail-swish of innocence -
too wise
to leave her free.

Piercing her surface with their spikes of hope and falsity,
their language reaches out to make her
bleed instead of be.

And so she struggles forward like a goldfish in a storm,
choking streams of questions
gill-by-gill she's being torn.

She mimics for the eye the tumbling,
choking,
downward cycle,
but hidden in the waves
fate wears her like a smile.

Drenching her senses
with their crash of theory and industry,
they warn her
it is only a mental mirror that she sees.

And so she struggles forward like a goldfish in a storm,
knowing that they cannot cage her ever-flowing form.

This equilibrium they are forcing
fails to balance or slow:
she knows this sea-struggle is but a mask
hiding their fears of long-ago.
She has no inner turbulence.
No battle of me against me.
She just reminds them of how sublime
and yet insignificant they can be.

And so she struggles forward like a goldfish needing air
but elsewhere she is merely
washing goldfish from her hair.

Babushka:

I have created a whole being

or perhaps she fell from me?

Little pieces of me that could not stay contained so they

spilled over

and bred whilst falling.

Either way, she is here with me now.

Little trinkets of me in her

and yet they are morphed treasures all of her own.

A loop within a loop within a star balanced on the moon

we are Babushka dolls.

Mid-cycle

a cosmic file

offering the traditions of the universe

wax-sealed indefinitely.

She is a labyrinth sketched in purple ink dripping from the stars.

I seek my answers in her book:

are you the echo of a perfect sunset

sinking

into my scope?

Are you my tip-toeing in midnight cloaks?

My thirst without fear and sad realisation

tickling at the throat?

Oh!

Perhaps she is the latter without the thirst to conquer it all!

Gods of the floor: I pray she isn't hopeless.

But breathe

right now in her youth she is

unscathed

untainted

untouched

and unaffected

completely self-contained.

So I knit and purl a new worry: she is my clarity

my awakening

my eventual knowing smile -

I will forever be held at a distance from myself

wandering mile after cosmic mile.

So she is my truth

and I cling to my child

like a child

with a mother's knowing smile.

Night Owl:

Using the sky as her canvass she dipped her hands
in bohemian ink
and tried to paint the taste of the truth hanging
on the tip of her tongue.

Never realising that up there
on her high-rise
she was closer to where she had begun;
only ever hide-seeking into herself
always fading before the sun.

Up there she thought she was levitating
but was really just seeped in a honey jar of her own
solitude.
The earth's shine reflecting on the darkest part
of the moon
was as close as she'd ever let herself get;
for the pain of the days
that always felt somehow broken -
like a gaping wound in the earth,
threatened to break her in the same way.

But the owl could see
what high-risers high-flyers high-achievers
were never tempted to see
and shone in her direction:
moving her searching blind eyes away

from decoding the smoke signals

of her own mind

towards now

unknowingly searching for feathers.

She a magpie, the owl a grounded star.

Now her fingers that had always reached for the moon

changed direction

and became fingers that craved to stroke air.

The owl became her magic dragon,

coming to her like precision personified:

like the second hand to the minute and the hour

the owl located her

and gave meaning to her movements.

A fan of feathers creating a sacred circle

whereby one leans, the other falls

the next cushions the descent of the

fallen -

lean, fall, support, like dominoes.

And so she leaned into the owl, healing in its glow.

The pipe she once smoked was now a feathered quill

scribbling the fable

of her heritage, her existence

and her foresight -

a story within a story

committed to the crumbling pages

of this owl-gifted paper moon.

She now no longer looked at this world

through a rippling puddle,

for the owl swooped in different colours:

not grey!

ivory lips whispering

a tapestry of colours

in between the black and white

that she had always seen.

Always spinning anti-clockwise

in this clockwise globe,

the owl taught her how to just be in this world

out

of

joint.

The owl held before her

the blueprint to a side of herself

that she had never given air to

and so she finally exhaled:

she opened her mouth and the glowing ashes of her past

scattered into the sky

becoming just another flickering of light

dispersed by the flap of an owl wing.

Now she sees her stepping-stones

as she watches the sunrise in the owl's eyes

with her bluest eye that once saw green

and now just sees feathers.

This high-rise girl is flying.

☾

Puddles:

Puddle side-stepping but inevitably
splashing.
It used to be a once-every-five-years-job
but now my socks are often sodden.
And it doesn't matter how much I prepare:
with the thick boots
or wellies
and farmers' socks
made out of industrial fibre or animal hair -

my toes are pruning and I know it is spreading.
The wild child in me tells me to
jump, splash, roar, repeat!
My reflection tells me
stop!
retreat!
Light that fire and phone indoorsy friends
puddles are not for you.
But they glisten and I smile recklessly.

The Barefoot Dancer

And so it came to be that a girl with hair as red as rage
climbed out of an apple of shallow green.

She touched the earth,
she was the earth,
cross-legged
this collage of a girl once unseen.

Reading from a crumbling book
that scholars had long forgotten,
she's just out of sight
blurred
like chalk on pavestone
dripping from puddle-splash
as you zip on by.
This girl glows with tequila raindrops.

Page-flicking
with hands like porcelain,
she throws the worlds' bad fortune
over her left shoulder and watches the grains
tumble
like gifts to the gods of the floor.
She scatters you, sprinkles you and reaches into your cosmic core.

You see, she is the kind of girl
who locates her soul
on her eighth eyelash in, top right.
Blotting at the cosmos
the stars striptease for her
as she stripteases for you -
performing a cabaret of the most enchanted kind,
this barefoot dancer with a wandering mind.

Crumbling and rolling and licking
the softest parts of you
whisper her name.

Put her in your pocket – quick –
while she's still
high and dry and tame.
And so you pass her melody around the room
like a hippy with a joint
and she comes to you like pieces of a loose dream.

Seeing for miles through her eyes
you unwire
dissolve
like scattered fireflies
as you mingle with her green genie to the boogie woogie beat.

This rainy day woman
is a prankster of time
and she holds you now in her palm:
a bosom full of fish
a long-stemmed wish
and barefoot dancing in moonshine.
Inhale her deeply
swallow her down.

Caressing beams that have deviated from a rainbow,
she eases your way –
life support
allowing you to peek through her fingertips of magic and clay.

Eyelashes now touching and blinking ceases to be
as she begins her slow sweet salsa,
dancing all over your body
like a gypsy lost at sea.

And finally, when you are dazed from the gaze of
the truth spoken
by this bitch dressed in language and smoke-rings,
and totally spent
with spirit trembling
and mind parched;
she turns her back on you
and illuminates you
as the sun illuminates the clouds
as it sinks away on the breath of the eve.

With gaping throat she leaves you
drifting towards sleep-hood,
her foot-falls
fading
fast.
Writing as a constant reminder of who she is,
this barefoot dancer was never meant to last.
Biting dust.

Alchemy

I knit a pedestal

for my babushka dolls

high above the spin of everything else -

tales of tea and toast.

They inherit my alchemy

I inherit the earth.

Plays from the Rooftop Ramblings collection

The Morning Lady:

As the scene opens the stage is lit with a tranquil, enveloping, soft orange hue. The 'warmth' is coming from the window they see centre downstage. The sun is slowly rising over the city landscape and the window is oversized and bare – no curtains, just venetian blinds rolled right up.

The warm glow illuminates The Morning Lady. She is scrooched down in a vintage embroidered wicker chair, left of the window, with her legs resting on the coffee table in front of her. On the table alongside her shoe-less feet is a cafetiere of steaming coffee, a small turquoise milk jug, a weighty glass ashtray and a small yellow tin. In her left hand she holds a steaming mug of said coffee and in her right hand she holds a spliff. Smoke billows lazily from the spliff in her hand and smoke-rings bounce across the room from her mouth to an unknown target.

She is in her late twenties or thirties or forties and dressed casually in inky black. She is a salt of the earth kind of girl; lounging in the sun reading, tapping her foot to a beat.

Suddenly there is a faint jangling of keys and The Man Who Doesn't Exist appears upstage right. He is in his early forties or fifties, wears a dark suit and is exceptionally well groomed. He is greying, wears his hair short and likes neither of these forced choices. He carries a leather briefcase and a matching holdall and looks like he's been tired for a very long time.

He is a man of the city and he likes things just the way he likes them.

The Man Who Doesn't Exist notices The Morning Lady, who has turned her head to look at him, mid smoke-ring. Confusion washes over his face and he scopes the room out briefly, confirming that he is indeed in the right flat and assessing possible danger.

The Morning Lady: (with slight caution) Hello?

The Man Who Doesn't' Exist: (stunned) Hello. What? Sorry, who are you?

The Morning Lady: (playfully) Perhaps I should be asking you the same thing! Do you live here?

The Man Who Doesn't Exist: Indeed! (Sergeant Major-esque) I repeat: Who are you?

The Morning Lady: I'm your cleaner.

The statement hangs in the air for a moment as The Man Who Doesn't Exist registers the information and confirms its plausibility. He nods to himself.

The Man Who Doesn't Exist: Right. I see, (pause) sorry, what are you doing here?

The Morning Lady: I'm cleaning (slight pause, then manically). Well not literally, I mean I'm not cleaning now. But I was. Look! (she sweeps her spliff-holding hand in the general direction of the room)Clean!

The Man Who Doesn't Exist glances around the room, unsure what he's supposed to be looking at, and then turns his attention back to The Morning Lady. He watches her, dumb-struck, as she takes the opportunity to toke on her spliff.

The Man Who Doesn't Exist: What is that? What are you doing? Is that a *joint?*

The Morning Lady: (wiggling her spliff in between her fingers and smiling) This? Yes.

36

Would you like some? And coffee! Come and sit down and have a smoke and a coffee with me. I don't have any croissants today, I'm afraid, but we do have the best bit to come - (she indicates towards the window, sun still slowly rising) Come.

She stands up and walks across the room to fetch another mug. The Man Who Doesn't Exist watches her, clearly in a state of utter bafflement. He pats his pockets, as if some kind of answer may be located there. She returns and pours him a coffee. He edges towards the sofa on the opposite side of the table and studies The Morning Lady as if she is on day release. She looks up at him amidst the aromatic steam of the coffee.

The Morning Lady: (graciously) Sit! Please.

He drops his bag and cautiously sits on the sofa, looking around him manically as if his world is about to fall apart. While she is making his coffee he studies her spliff in the ashtray.

The Man Who Doesn't Exist: (shocked and annoyed) An ashtray? You bought your own ashtray!

The Morning Lady: No, (pause) this is *your* ashtray…

The Man Who Doesn't Exist: (scoffing) *My* Ashtray!

The Morning Lady: Yes. This is *your* ashtray that I got from *your* kitchen cupboard (she nods in the general direction of the kitchen). Don't worry, I always wash it thoroughly and put it back.

The Man Who Doesn't Exist: (embarrassed, back-tracking) Right. Yes. Well done. I don't smoke, not really, you see. My secretary – she organised the flat and all in it. I suppose it's for guests – the ashtray.

The Morning Lady: (playfully) And the flat also?

The Man Who Doesn't Exist: What?

With a slight smile, The Morning Lady lets the question slide. Now both with coffee in hand, she pulls the wicker chair to her and sits again, immediately looking towards the glowing window with visible calm washing over her. Utter annoyance flashes in The Man Who Doesn't Exist: he places his coffee cup firmly on the table and points at the chair.

You even brought your own chair! I cannot believe it! (standing) You come here and you look out of *my* window with your coffee and your *drugs* and your socks (he points towards her flamboyantly odd socks) and you even have the audacity to bring your own *bastard* chair!

The Morning Lady tries to interject but he holds his hand up and continues rambling, now with complete melt-down potential rising in his voice. His hand movements become sketchy and he begins to pace.

I mean, who bloody lives here? (thumping his chest in recognition) Me! *I* live here and this is *my* window! (gesturing towards the table) These are *my* cups and this is *my* coffee – hang on – *is* this my coffee? (he calms quickly with the question and then gets het up again when she nods). This is *my* coffee and you pour it as freely as if it's your own! You do all this and you make me feel like I'm going bloody crazy (he pulls at his hair) and then you cherry it by bringing your own *bastard* chair!

The Morning Lady: (unfazed and blowing smoke towards the window) This is *your* bastard chair.

The Man Who Doesn't Exist: (eyes wide, confusion flickering all about him) What?

The Morning Lady: This is *your* bastard chair.

The Man Who Doesn't Exist: (stunned and dropping to almost a whisper) *My* bastard chair?

The Morning Lady: Indeedy. This is *your* chair and it resides in *your* guest room (she motions with her head behind her towards the guest room and takes another drag on her spliff).

The Man Who Doesn't Exist looks around tentatively and then edges over to peek in to the guest room.

The Man Who Doesn't Exist: (in utter dismay) It isn't in keeping with anything! It's in my guest room… (he trails off and when he next speaks his tone is one of utter resignation.) Oh for fuck's sake!

He walks over to the sofa and again seats himself opposite The Morning Lady. He loosens his tie, takes off his suit jacket and accepts the spliff that The Morning Lady extends to him, like a house-warming gift.

The Morning Lady: You ok?

The Man Who Doesn't Exist: (exhaling a billowing puff of smoke) Do you really care?

The Morning Lady: Of course I do. If you drop down dead from stress who on earth will I clean for?

He smiles and she returns it. He takes another toke and then hands her the spliff.

The Man Who Doesn't Exist: So, cleaning hey! Do you enjoy it?

The Morning Lady: (in between tokes) Well, I enjoy cleaning your flat, if that's what you can call it. I mean, there's barely any trace that you live here! No photos, no cushions, no mess. I don't have to do that much on the cleaning front, but as you can see; I have a nice little routine going on here. (she sweeps her hands across the table, motioning to all her bits and bobs scattered there) Yes I do enjoy it, thanks. And what is it you do exactly (she hands the spliff back to him) that requires you to hardly be here, not know what's in your guest room or where you keep you coffee?

The Man Who Doesn't Exist: Funny. I'm a banking consultant.

The Morning Lady: (scoffs and winks at him)

The Man Who Doesn't Exist: Funny fucker aren't you! I'm out of the country for at least a few days every week so no, I'm not really in touch with what goes on around here.

The Morning Lady: Nice work if you can get it.

The Man Who Doesn't Exist: Isn't it. Why don't you think about getting some qualifications behind you and going for your peach job? Something a bit more stimulating?

The Morning Lady: You assume that I've not got any qualifications or that I lack stimulation? Why, my friend, I do believe this is not your area of expertise and you are therefore not qualified enough to pass judgement on me.

The Man Who Doesn't Exist: (indignantly) I am qualified!

The Morning Lady: To discuss topics of stimulation?

The Man Who Doesn't Exist: Well, no. Maybe. Not stimulation perhaps…

The Morning Lady: (cutting him off) No, you're not. My dear, I do believe this is the most stimulated you have been in a very long time, and that's thanks to me. So I win and I hold the qualifications.

The Man Who Doesn't Exist: (matter-of-factly) Don't get me wrong, I can tell you're an intelligent woman. But really, how qualified must one be to clean?

The Morning Lady: More qualified and skilled than you, evidently, seeing as you pay me to do it for you!

The Man Who Doesn't Exist: Aha! But isn't that just a little luxury of mine? It doesn't mean I can't do it.

The Morning Lady: (mimicking his tone) Aha! Can you?

The Man Who Doesn't Exist: Can I what?

The Morning Lady: Clean.

The Man Who doesn't Exist: Well of course I can!

The Morning Lady: What would you use to clean this table?

The Man Who doesn't Exist: A cloth. Of some sort. Yes - a cloth. (justifyingly) Well look, it's as simple as being shown how to do it and then I would know, wouldn't I?!

The Morning Lady: Yes, and if you show me how to consult on banking then I would be able to do that, wouldn't I?

The Man Who doesn't Exist. Fair point, well made. (pause) I just mean, isn't there something else you'd like to do?

The Morning Lady: Not right now. No. And besides, I like cleaning your flat, if you can even call it that - cleaning I mean. I do more cleaning up after myself around here than I do after you! Hmmm I guess that makes you even stupider than I thought, seeing as you pay me to watch the sunrise through reefer smoke.

The Man Who Doesn't Exist: You're making yourself redundant here! And why am I more stupid? Stupider? When was I just stupid?

The Morning Lady: (chuckling) Well that whole 'your *bastard* chair' episode was pretty stupid.

The Man Who Doesn't Exist: (bashfully) Quite.

The Morning Lady: And as a point of reference, I I have a Masters. (The Morning Lady holds his gaze for a moment and then excitedly turns towards the window and points) Look! This is my favourite part.

He considers her for a moment and then follows her gaze. Sitting in silence they watch the sun peek over the top of St Paul's Cathedral. After a moment he turns back to her.

The Man Who Doesn't Exist: You watch the sunrise every time you're here?

The Morning Lady: (nodding and smiling somewhat timidly) To be honest, it's the main reason I'm still doing it.

The Man Who Doesn't Exist: The cleaning? For the sunrise?

She again nods and for the first time since their encounter looks small and fragile.

But you don't have to come here to see the sun rise… (trailing off)

The Morning Lady: The time and space is peaceful – it's therapeutic for me here, just having time to myself to smoke, drink and watch the sunrise. I know I can do that at home, or anywhere else for that matter, but I don't feel so lonely here, just kind of seeped in solitude instead - (they catch each other's eye and hold it) do you understand?

The Man Who Doesn't Exist: Indeed. (long pause as he considers their places in the world) It's funny isn't it: I on the other hand *always* feel lonely when I'm here and can't wait to be travelling again. Different strokes for different folks and all that.

The Morning Lady: (with a quietly serious tone) I don't think we're that different really. (changing the subject and brightening her tone) You know, the views from here are tremendous – you could make a killing if you sub-let it. I mean you're barely here at all.

The Man Who Doesn't Exist: By all accounts I should be sub-letting to you! You live here more than I do!

The Morning Lady: (softly and without offense meant) Or perhaps just live more?

They stare at each other pensively for a moment, his eyes breaking away first.

Do you want another coffee?

The Man Who Doesn't Exist: Sure.

He reaches over and examines her 'smoking' tin and its contents whilst accepting the diminishing spliff back from her.

The Morning Lady: (pouring more coffee) So what's with you getting your secretary to kit your flat out? How did you know you'd like her style? Have you known her long?

The Man Who Doesn't Exist: She's been my secretary for about….um… six years now.

The Morning Lady: And? (prompting him) Why did you trust her interior decorating skills?

The Man Who Doesn't Exist: (after a moment of reflection) She's clean. She always looks *clean.*

The Morning Lady: (giggling) And what, that covers a whole general 'dirty' category does it? (she hands him fresh coffee and then resumes her position on the wicker chair).

The Man Who Doesn't Exist: (tittering slightly, seeing the funny side) Yes I suppose it does. It worked (he waves his hand in the general 'flat' direction). It all looks clean.

The Morning Lady: And that would have nothing to do with me then?

The Man Who Doesn't Exist: Oh right. Indeed.

There is a comfortable silence as The Morning Lady rolls another spliff.

So when you're done for the day and put your glad rags and heels on, whereabouts do you normally wreak your havoc?

The Morning Lady: (scoffing) Heels! I smoke too much weed to even balance in trainers! (she extends her leg and wiggles her 'flamboyant' toes) Do you know, when you first walked in I thought you were an estate agent showing the flat! I had a real Scooby-Doo moment where I did a double-take…

They giggle and the chatter continues to a faint nothing as the house lights fade. After a slight interlude, the house lights rise again, revealing that it is now night. The Man Who Doesn't Exist is moving about the flat on his own. His travelling bags are by the door and he is wearing his trademark dark suit. He walks into the guest room and returns with the wicker chair that The Morning Lady favours, and puts it next to the window. He then moves in the direction of the kitchen and returns with a plate of croissants and the ashtray. He positions them on the table for The Morning Lady's next visit, scoops up his keys, briefly checks his surroundings and leaves with a satisfied smile.

End:

The Pistachio Thief.

*As the scene opens the audience is presented
with a very 'lived-in' (if not a tad messy)
front-room. Stage left and angled so the
audience can see it fully, is a sofa with a tie-
dyed hippy throw over it. In front of the sofa
is a coffee table strewn with glasses, mugs,
empty bottles and a bong; it is clearly the
aftermath of a party or gathering of sorts.
On the other side of the coffee table is a games
console with controls attached. A lava lamp
glows in the room, although the room is well lit
and all of its contents can be seen.*

*Down stage right there is an open window,
through which the audience can see it is dark
outside, although there is no other indication
of time. Right of the window is a cabinet with a
stereo on it. There are CDs scattered all over
and around the stereo – the effect is that they
are breeding across the front-room.*

*Destroying the stillness of the room is a man
easing himself through the open window and
entering the front-room. He moves slowly and
cautiously and keeps his eyes on the room in
front of him. He is Pilfering Paddy and this is
perhaps his first time pilfering: he wears jeans
and a bright t-shirt and he bangs his head on
the window frame as he sneaks inside.*

Pilfering Paddy: (ducking his head down and
rubbing the sprouting bump) Shit, shit, shit!

*Realising his indiscretion, he moves his hand
from his head to instead cover his mouth, as if
to comically silence himself. He momentarily
pauses and checks the room again before easing
himself fully through the window. His feet hit a
pile of the scattered CDs and he stumbles.*

46

Fuck, shit, fuck!

He jumps up quickly and stands motionless with panic painted across his face. After a few seconds he slowly tip-toes to the stereo and starts trying to unplug it. In his fumbling he accidentally hits the play button and the room booms with the song 'London Calling' by The Clash. Pilfering Paddy jumps back in horror. He begins to move towards the window and then changes his mind. He reaches out to the stereo in a feeble attempt to silence it, changes his mind and again moves towards the window, before turning back to the stereo one final time.

(hands on his head in camp despair) No, no, no, bugger!

As the lyrics begin to bounce across the room, a man enters upstage left. He sings along to the song and rhythmically walks, perhaps he even jigs, across the room and towards Pilfering Paddy. The jigging, swaying, singing man wears grubby frayed jeans, flip-flops and a bright Hawaiian shirt partially unbuttoned. His hair hangs lazily about his face and he has a broad smile as he sings. He is Stoner Sam and he sees daffodils instead of debts, rainbows instead of rain, and he speaks with a deep Southern American drawl.

Stoner Sam: (singing) London calling to the faraway towns! Now war is declared and battle come down! London calling to the underworld! Come out of the cupboard, you boys and girls!

As Stoner Sam faces Pilfering Paddy the music drops to a comfortable warble.

Dude! What a fucking tune, man! I didn't realise there was anyone still here.

Pilfering Paddy: (confused and clearly struggling with the unexpected intrusion) What?

Stoner Sam: (still smiling broadly and with a hint of a chuckle) Been a rough one for you too, hey? I thought everyone had left, man. (pausing and ruffling his hair as if trying to shake a bit of reality back in to himself) And to my embarrassment, dear friend, I have forgotten all of my manners along with your name…(extending his hand to Pilfering Paddy) Sam, nice to meet you… again! Probably for the umpteenth time tonight (chuckles)

Pilfering Paddy: (cautiously shaking Stoner Sam's hand) Yeah man, yeah… Paddy.

Stoner Sam: Good. Like I said, it's been a long night. There were that many faces here tonight it looked like a scene from Woodstock!

Pilfering Paddy: (clearly not understanding the reference) Yeah. Yeah, man. Cool.

There is a long pause as Stoner Sam eyes Pilfering Paddy, almost mischievously.

So what (nodding towards the stereo) you dig this shit, man?

Stoner Sam: The Clash? Well honestly, I couldn't say a bad word against them, my friend, except perhaps that they don't record anymore, but shit I guess they have their reasons. A bit like the woman I love no longer wanting to be pleasured. I'm sure she could sit me down and give me a hundred and one valuable reasons that I could relate to and none of them would be about me personally and none of them would be understandable from my viewpoint. Doesn't mean I don't miss it, but I can't complain about shit that I can't do shit about. What can I say? Dig?

Pilfering Paddy: (looking around him in total confusion) What? What?

Stoner Sam: Come again! Exactly my thoughts. So seeing as you're clearly not a Clash man, for which I will have to educate your ass later on, what is it you were looking for? (nods towards the stereo)

Pilfering Paddy: (flustered) You'll have to do what to my ass?

Stoner Sam: (ignoring Pilfering Paddy's slight confrontation) Music. What do you want?

Pilfering Paddy: Nothing. No man I'm cool. I'm good just here, chilling.

Stoner Sam: You don't like music, maestro? You don't want to pick a tune or two, like a musical Fagin? (chuckles to himself)

Pilfering Paddy: What? Fay-who? Music? Of course, man. Music be the food of life and all that. Yeah I like music, shit! But nah, man, you wouldn't know it. Nah, I'm old school you know and my modern stuff is a bit underground. Nah you wouldn't… (trailing off and again looking awkward)

Stoner Sam: Come on, dude. I can be mole-like, all underground and shit. (slight pause whilst they eye each other up) Bet you a toke I can surprise you, my friend. (excitedly now) Bet you a toke! What would you listen to right now if you had a choice? Name that tune… (he karate chops the air, or conducts, or something similar)

Pilfering Paddy: (uncomfortable) Nah, just leave it, man. You've made it a big deal now. All awkward and shit (kissing his teeth)

Stoner Sam: Come on, dude, just say it! You're acting like a bitch now and I ain't about to buy you flowers. (chuckles) Name that tune. Tick, tock, tick, tock….

Pilfering Paddy: (annoyed) People Under the Stairs, man! Tick, tock, tick, tock, shit, Motherfucker! Yeah! There! People Under the Stairs, and then I'd be educating your ass! (calming again) But nah, forget it, man.

Stoner Sam smiles cheekily at Pilfering Paddy, strolls over to the sofa singing and turning to point in Pilfering Paddy's direction.

Stoner Sam: (singing) We don't need no education! (rummages in the sofa cushions and then produces a CD) Teacher! Leave those kids alone! (he waves the CD at Pilfering Paddy and stops singing) There is clearly no teacher here, man.

Pilfering Paddy steps forward slightly and cranes to see the CD.

You owe me a toke, man. You owe me a toke! (chuckles heavily and beams like the Cheshire Cat)

Pilfering Paddy: What the fuck! Get out of town! (looking at the CD again) No? No! You're like a fucking magician! What else you got in that sofa?

Stoner Sam again jigs across the front room to the stereo and puts the CD on.

Stoner Sam: (comically bowing slightly) May I make the selection?

Pilfering Paddy waves his hand towards Stoner Sam in a royal fashion and Stoner Sam presses 'play' on the stereo. They both stand motionless, heads back in musical bliss as the introduction to 'Acid Raindrops' by People Under the Stairs begins to play. They make appreciative eye contact, a few complimentary gestures are thrown, and both breathe deeply, as if the melodies are tickling their spines and clearing their heads. They jig around the room; each in their own separate styles, but with a shared musical appreciation, as lyrics float around the room like bubbles.

Both Singing: Let's have a mid-city fiesta with your west LA connections, hop inside the vehicle, start crossing intersections. We learning life's lessons while we blaze this herbal essence, a man was still a child and I have so many questions.

As the music continues, they both sway and sing in mutually appreciative harmony. Stoner Sam two-steps over to the sofa and starts dragging deeply on his bong. Smoke billows across the room. Pilfering Paddy joins Stoner Sam on the sofa and accepts the bong from him. They sink in to the sofa in unison and exhale deeply; Pilfering Paddy releasing smoke, Stoner Sam releasing bad vibes.

Pilfering Paddy: (nodding briefly in Stoner Sam's direction and momentarily catching his eye) I'm impressed, man. A stoner with taste and a touch of wisdom.

Stoner Sam: Are you kidding me? A stoner always has taste! How else do you explain the insatiable munchies? And for your information, my dear newly acquainted friend, I may only be wearing flip-flops, my shirt may only be fastened with a safety pin and there may be nothing more than ice-cubes in my freezer, but a stoner always has clarity because (motioning towards the room, his weed, the music) I live with Mary Jane and her eyes are as green as the

Emerald City – don't those freaky fucks all look for wisdom in the Emerald City? Ha! (smugly) Indeedy my friend: I have Mary Jane, I have wisdom. Case rested.

Pilfering Paddy: (with a dubious then whole-hearted smile) You're the Wizard!

Stoner Sam eyes up Pilfering Paddy, clearly figuring out whether to take the comment seriously or not. He arches an eyebrow and they both get the insatiable giggles. There then follows lots of mutually appreciative glances, juvenile arm punches and the passing back and forth of the bong until they finally wipe the giggle tears from their eyes and slowly fall silent. A long pause follows, but it is by no means an uncomfortable one.

You're ok man. Respect. Seriously.

Stoner Sam: (singing) R.E.S.P.E.C.T! Find out what it means to me!

More brief giggling

Pilfering Paddy: You can't go wrong with a bit of Aretha. (looking around the room whilst toking) So, nice gaff, man, nice. You live here alone?

Stoner Sam: Yep. Just me, myself and I. Although to be perfectly honest, Sire, I honestly can't remember the last time I didn't have company. I mean, even when there's no-one here it's like a scene from One Flew over the Cuckoo's nest! (chuckles to himself) You know?

Pilfering Paddy: (looks confused, attempts to say something, looks confused again and then concedes) Um no. But yeah, man, I get that like you're busy and shit, yeah?

Stoner Sam: That I am, my friend, that I am. As busy as a bee on speed. (toking) How's about you?

Pilfering Paddy: Yeah I'm busy, man, but not so much with people, ya know? I feel like I'm always busy trying to make money, but there's not much of it to show for my efforts. (philosophically) But I do try, man, and I guess that's the important thing. But I get lonely, shit of course I do.

Stoner Sam: I meant to enquire about your domestic arrangements - where you live, if you co-habit and so forth, but shit you jumped that one step beyond and came up with some honest to God bullshit right there! An honest man - I like that! You went further and jumped ahead - you're like a fucking time traveller man!

Pilfering Paddy: I'm Doc

Stoner Sam: You are Doc! God Damn! That must make me Marty!

Both Singing: Don't need money, don't take fame. Don't need no credit card to ride this train. It's strong and it's sudden and it's cruel sometimes, but it might just save your life. That's the power of love!

They fall about laughing again

Pilfering Paddy: I never looked at it like that, man. I am a fucking time traveller and you are the Wizard of the Emerald City.

Stoner Sam: What a fine pair!

Pilfering Paddy: I'll smoke to that!

They smoke

Stoner Sam: So you try real hard at various things – that's a good philosophy, my friend, but people are good to bounce off you know? You need more people, you see, because you appear to be good at bouncing – in fact you're like one big bloody ball! I say you bounce more.

Pilfering Paddy: Yeah I hear that, Wizard, I hear that. Although spending a lot of time on my own gives me time to think, you know. Keeps the cogs turning and all that. And talking of bouncing (he checks his watch and nods towards the door)

Stoner Sam: It's a fair comment from a fair man – cogs are always at their best when they're turning. So now you have to bounce, but have it be known that my door is always open if you ever want to bounce a bit… (slight pause) Or indeed my window…

Pilfering Paddy: What?

Stoner Sam: Man, if you wanted the stereo, or indeed needed it, then you only had to ask. I'm a fellow that believes that if you don't ask, you don't get, you know?

Pilfering Paddy: (with shocked embarrassment and shame) Ah shit. I didn't mean…… Ah shit. Shit. (he fidgets and fumbles and stumbles over his words)

Stoner Sam: Listen Doc, I don't give a flying monkey's fanny what your intentions were when you came in my window. I have genuinely enjoyed your company and you can bounce through my window or my door any time you so desire. I sincerely mean that, dude (he places his hand over his heart to indicate sincerity)

Pilfering Paddy: (still embarrassed) Shit. You knew all along?

Stoner Sam: (nodding) And I stand by my word: If you need the stereo you can take it. It's yours. But! Think about this…

Pilfering Paddy: (interrupting Stoner Sam) I don't want the stereo man, shit!

Stoner Sam: Think about this Doc: If you need that stereo more than I need Aretha, then by all means take it. It's your question to answer, your stereo if you so please.

Pilfering Paddy: (looking at Stoner Sam in quiet appreciation) Nobody needs that stereo as much as you need Aretha, man, and I mean that from the bottom of my heart. Respect. (pause) I should really shift and see a man about a dog.

Stoner Sam: Indeedy fine friend, indeedy. Understood. But I personally only ever see men about the truth, but each to their own and all that. A parting toke?

Pilfering Paddy: In the words of a great man (mimics the Southern drawl) Indeedy, my friend, indeedy.

They both resume their places on the sofa and the smoke thickens, the music is turned up and the lights fade, until all you can see is the bubbling lava lamp.

End:

Mims and the Moon

www.mimsandthemoon.com